Mr. Scootie

The Tale of a Little Dog from Chincoteague

Mr. Scootie

The Tale of a Little Dog from Chincoteague

Written & Illustrated By

Sarita A. Cooke

Osprey Island Press

About the Cover Painting: The cover is an oil pastel of a Chincoteague sunset by the author.

Mr. Scootie

Copyright © 2010 by Sarita A. Cooke

ISBN: 978-0-615-37565-6

Osprey Island Press
10 Hurlingham Club Road
Far Hills, NJ 07931

www.OspreyIslandPress.com

PRINTED IN THE UNITED STATES OF AMERICA

This story is for Elise, Penelope and Daphne

Mr. Scootie

The Tale of a Little Dog from Chincoteague

Mr. Scootie

A long time ago, a little white dog named Mr. Scootie lived on a very special island where, for hundreds of years, wild ponies grazed on the marsh grass and galloped along the wide sandy beaches beside the Atlantic Ocean. The ponies had became so famous that every year people from all over the world came to see them.

When night fell, covering the island with its inky black cape, the visitors were always amazed and filled with wonder, because above them trillions of teeny little yellow stars twinkled and sparkled in the sky; but the stars were an island secret, and nobody ever told the visitors about Mr. Scootie, the little white dog who knew how to fly.

The islanders also didn't tell them that he usually came back to the island every day and that only the children could still see him, because Mr. Scootie now lived on a star high up in the sky.

It was on clear nights, in the brief moment between dusk and darkness that he usually flew back to his star, after he'd spent a busy day on the island visiting Mr. and Mrs. Bean, with whom he had lived with for most of his life. As he flew above the little fishermen's cottages the children would peep through their curtains, hoping to catch a glimpse of him.

If they were lucky enough to see him, they opened their windows and sent him lots of kisses from the tips of their fingers. The gentle evening breeze then carried them high up into the sky, as if it too knew the children's secret: that when their kisses landed on Mr. Scootie's furry white coat they turned into bright little yellow stars.

Mr. Scootie was glad that his star wasn't too far from the island. He missed Mr. and Mrs. Bean so much that he tried to visit them every day, if the weather was good enough for him to land safely. At first, when he flew back, he heard Mrs. Bean making little sniffly noises like she was crying, and that made him feel all sad and sniffly too.

Mr. Bean kept telling her that Mr. Scootie had gone to live in a lovely happy place, and that he would still be able to visit them, even if they couldn't see him any longer. But Mrs. Bean said she didn't believe him, and she didn't want to hear about the happy place where Mr. Scootie had vanished to. She just wanted him to come right back and sit all cuddlebug on her lap again.

When Mr. Scootie heard that, he was so happy he flew up and gave her a lovely wet lick on her cheek. At first Mrs. Bean cried out, saying. "Oh my, oh, my, I think, well I think something just touched my cheek, and it's wet." So Mr. Scootie kept licking her cheek until, in a magical moment, she turned to Mr. Bean and said, "Mr. Scootie couldn't be giving me kisses?"

"Oh yes, indeed he could, I told you he was still with us," replied Mr. Bean.

Then Mrs. Bean started to laugh, "Oh how wonderful, how absolutely wonderful, and I can talk to him just as I always have," she said giving Mr. Bean a big hug. Mr. Scootie was so happy he stood up on his hind legs and did his special twirly dance that always created a little breeze. When Mrs. Bean finally felt it she looked down laughing and said, "Oh, I felt that my dear, dear Mr. Scootie. Welcome home. And promise me you will always give me a kiss to let me know when you are here."

Mr. Scootie also wondered if Mrs. Bean's cats knew when he came back to visit. They had never liked him, and they were both bigger than he was so they always gave him the shivvies. Both of them seemed to enjoy circling around him

hissing and growling. Mr. Huggybug often smacked him on the nose for no reason while Miss Peekaboo would hide behind doors, and when he was busy chasing his toys, she'd jump out of nowhere, frightening him to death; then she'd vanish faster than a ghost.

But as he'd grown older and no longer barked and ran around the house chasing his toys, they seemed to like him much better. They even enjoyed sleeping with him on his soft green bed in the kitchen.

Mr. Scootie never understood what had happened to him on the night he had flown away. It was just an ordinary night, and he was fast asleep and all tuckabug with Mr. Huggybug and Miss Peekaboo when he felt something strange happening to his ears. At first they twitched and stood up like two little white rockets. Then he felt them growing longer and longer, and before he knew what was happening, he was flying up through the roof of his house and out into the inky black sky. Although his ears hurt and his legs were making funny twirly motions, he didn't have time to feel frightened because he was going too fast.

Then, just as he was getting the hang of flying, he landed on something soft and purple in the sky. Although his legs collapsed beneath him, his body kept skidding across the purple grass until he bumped into a very large rock. He hurt his nose, and his body ached so badly he started to sniffle. But he was sure that soon Mrs. Bean would come and pick him up. She always cuddled him when he had dreams that made him sniffle and bark.

Yet there was something about this dream that felt different from all the others he'd had. As he lay panting with exhaustion and pain, everything was completely silent, but Mr. Scootie was too tired and frightened to move, and, within seconds, he fell fast asleep next to the nasty rock he'd bumped into.

He must have slept for a very long time because when he woke up, no matter

how hard he tried, he couldn't remember what had happened to him. Mrs. Bean was nowhere to be seen; he was still in this purple place and the sun was shining. He also realized that he wasn't lying in his bed with Mr. Huggybug and Miss Peekaboo having a horrid dream about flying, and that something very strange indeed was going on.

He tried to stand up but his legs went all wobbly and he kept falling over — his whole body ached, his fur was in a frightful mess and he was feeling terribly frightened. Finally, after a lot of tries, he managed to stand up and he hoped that a good roll about might make him feel better. So he rolled around and all about, scritching and scratching all his tickly bits, and he was busy shaking out his furry white coat, when he suddenly noticed that a very small mouse was watching him from a distance.

He was very startled because he'd never met a mouse before, but he thought he should be polite so he lifted a paw and said, "Hello." However, the mouse ignored him, started to clean its whiskers, and stared at him intently out of its two bright little beady black eyes. Mr. Scootie thought the mouse was being terribly rude and he started to cry. Suddenly, quicker than lightening, the mouse scampered up his back and swept his tears away with a tiny paw. Then it sat on the end of his nose and continued to clean its whiskers.

Mr. Scootie was afraid that the mouse might fall off his nose if he opened his mouth, so, in a whispery voice he asked it where he was. The mouse stopped cleaning her whiskers and told him that he had landed on a star. Then the mouse said, "Oh by the way, how do you do, I'm Miss Mouse, what's your name?"

"Er, um, well, um, I'm called Mr. Scootie," he replied, and when he turned his head around very slowly to have a look, he saw that trillions of stars were twinkling and sparkling all around him. He was so surprised he shook his head in

disbelief sending Miss Mouse flying off the end of his nose. He tried to apologize, but she dismissed him with the wave of a tiny paw and continued to clean her whiskers.

Mr. Scootie was so shocked that he just sat silently staring out at all the stars wondering how he had ended up sitting in the sky on a purple star talking to a mouse. He got such an attack of the shivvies that they made his teeth chatter. Eventually he calmed down enough to ask Miss Mouse why he was there. She gave him a beautiful smile, that showed off her two pointy white teeth, and told him in her squeaky voice that he'd just become a Fairy Dog. He didn't know what she was talking about and this time his tears splashed all over Miss Mouse, who didn't seem to mind one bit. She just shook out her little brown coat, sending his tears flying all around and about as they lit up the sky, glowing brightly like tiny fireflies.

"I'm a Fairy Dog?" he gasped.

"Yes, yes, you are, and I'm a Fairy Mouse," she replied, as if that explained everything, which of course, it didn't. Mr. Scootie knew a little bit about fairies because Mrs. Bean used to read stories about them to her grandchildren. But he thought fairies only lived in books and they always seemed to be pretty little girls with wings. He had never heard Mrs. Bean mention a Fairy Dog or a Fairy Mouse.

He was pondering all this very deeply when he heard a loud whoosh and an enormous bird with funny looking pointed ears landed next to Miss Mouse, ruffled its feathers, and asked her who the little white dog was. The big bird had the largest eyes Mr. Scootie had ever seen; they looked like two enormous yellow saucers with big black spots floating about in the middle of them. In fact, he wasn't even sure it was a bird because he'd never seen one with ears before.

"Heard you'd arrived," announced the strange bird. "Frightful gossips up here I'm afraid. What's your name little man?"

Mr. Scootie opened his mouth to reply but no sound came out. "Can't hear you, you've got to speak louder," said the long-eared bird.

"Can't," whispered Mr. Scootie, "I don't know what you are."

"I'm an Owl, my dear chap. Hoo hoo hoo, hoo hoo hoo."

"Oh gosh," thought Mr. Scootie; he was terrified of owls. Mrs. Bean used to take him out on special walkies at night. Often she'd suddenly stop and say, "Sssshhhhssh, did you hear that Mr. Scootie?" as a spooky "Hoo hoo hoo, hoo hoo hoo" would echo through the thick white fog. He never told her he was terrified of sounds he couldn't see and then, just as his shivvies began to calm down, he'd hear another dreadful schreeching sound and nearly jump out of his fur with fright. Mrs. Bean would get all excited telling him that he'd just heard a Screech Owl. But he didn't want to hear any more owl sounds; so he'd usually make a mad dash back to the safety of his soft green bed and the cats, Mr. Huggybug and Miss Peekaboo. "Well, well, well," he thought, "so this is what those scary sounding night birds looked like." They were certainly very odd looking and he didn't like being stared at by two such enormous yellow eyes.

"Hope you don't snore at night; can't abide snoring," said the Owl gruffly.

"Oh, do be kind," squeaked Miss Mouse. "He's terribly frightened, and you haven't introduced yourself properly," she scolded him.

"Well, I'm known as Mr. Owl," he replied. Then Miss Mouse told him that they should welcome Mr. Scootie properly. So Mr. Owl spread out his wings. Miss Mouse held onto one of his feathers, and they began to dance and sing:

> *You're in the land of the Golden Light, The Golden Light, The*
> *Golden Light; it's full of harmony and everything's bright,*
> *welcome to the land of The Golden Light.*

Despite this welcome, Mr. Scootie just wanted to leave the horrible star as soon as possible, so he asked them how long he had to stay before he could go back to his island. "Oh, you're here for good, dear chap," Mr. Owl told him.

"You mean I can't go back to my home ever again?" Mr. Scootie gasped, as more tears started to trickle down his face. And once again Miss Mouse dashed up his back and swept them away before they fell off his nose. But the sharp eyes of Mr. Owl had spotted his tears so, in a gentler voice, he said, "There, there, don't worry; of course you can go back. Most of us pop back and forth all the time."

"Well, not everybody," chimed in Miss Mouse. Mr. Owl gave her a loving look with his huge eyes and told Mr. Scootie that she hadn't been happy down there, living in the Green World; and he added, that he could understand Mr. Scootie's feelings. "I know all of this is a bit of a shock in the beginning, but you'll grow to love living here once you get used to it." Mr. Scootie doubted that he'd ever get used to living on a star, especially when it seemed that, only a few hours ago, he'd been fast asleep with Mr. Huggybug and Miss Peekaboo.

"Why do I have to stay here?" he asked, feeling both cross and scared at the same time.

"Well," replied Mr. Owl, "it's like this you see. We all live in the Green World for a while, then, when we become ancient, we have to leave it and so we come up here to live in the Golden World, just as you have." Mr. Owl puffed up his feathers making him look like a giant balloon.

"Why do you keep calling it the Green World?" asked Mr. Scootie.

"It's the trees, dear fellow. The place is covered with them," replied Mr. Owl. "Wonderful things trees; full of wisdom and some of them have been down there for thousands of years. In fact the Green World couldn't exist without them."

Mr. Owl went on to explain how trees made everything work properly by

filling the Green World with good air, while at the same time they took all the bad air away. "Because," Mr. Owl continued, "if there was only bad air in the Green World nothing would be able to live down there. Trees are marvelous things, truly marvelous." Mr. Owl fell silent remembering all the big trees and woods he'd flown through when he lived in the Green World, and the three of them sat in a row pondering the importance of trees.

Finally, Mr. Scootie broke the silence by asking Mr. Owl if he had to go back to the Green World as a dog. Mr. Owl looked at him sharply and said, "Well, yes. Most of us go back as ourselves. Why? What did you have in mind?" he asked.

"I've always wanted to be a bird," replied Mr. Scootie. Mr. Owl and Miss Mouse looked at him as if he'd just turned into a frog in front of their eyes. Mr. Owl puffed up all his feathers and said, "So you want to go back as a bird do you? What sort of bird did you have in mind?" But Mr. Scootie didn't want to tell him about his secret dream.

Every morning he used to sit on the dock with Mrs. Bean watching all the different marsh birds and, on occasion, a beautiful bird with enormous wings would fly across the cove, suddenly dive into the water and catch a fish. Mr. Scootie thought it was so beautiful, that he longed to launch himself out into the sky to join it.

Because it was a bigger bird than Mr. Owl, Mr. Scootie didn't want to hurt his feelings; so he just mumbled "Anosprey."

"Oh do speak more clearly," said Mr. Owl crossly, "I can't hear you. What sort of bird do you want to be?" But, just then, they were interrupted by a lot of squeaky noises, as Miss Mouse ran around in circles with her front paws clasped tightly to her ears. She always got nervous when she heard about birds, because in the Green World big birds, like Mr. Owl, would have tried to eat her, and she

Bald Eagle

hoped that Mr. Scootie didn't want to turn into a mouse-eating bird, because then it would be very difficult for her to be his friend.

Poor Miss Mouse never wanted to go anywhere near the Green World again. Nasty "see in the dark" birds chased her. And humans always screamed when they saw her and jumped on chairs, but she spent most of her time running away from cats. However, she never felt afraid up in the Golden World, because nobody needed to eat anything. "Do you really want to go back to the Green World?" she asked him. "Everything's so scary down there." Mr. Scootie had to agree with her because he'd lived in three different homes before Mrs. Bean found him, and changed his life.

Children had pulled his tail and teased him, while others shut him up in a small cage all day. Then, when they came home and let him out, he'd chew all their shoes up into little bits, but that made them so mad that they would take him back to the animal shelter, and leave him there again. He never had to stay there for very long, unlike most dogs, because Mrs. Bean told him that Maltese dogs, like him, were very special. She explained that for thousands of years, Kings and Queens had owned dogs just like him, and because they were little dogs, they could sit on their laps and that made the Kings and Queens very happy. But the only lap Mr. Scootie ever sat on was Mrs. Bean's, so he was sure she was the Queen of the wild pony island.

Mr. Scootie had been so busy with his memories that he nearly jumped out of his fur with fright when he heard Mr. Owl telling him gruffly that it would be very difficult to go back as a bird. Mr. Owl explained that he'd have to go in front of the Knowledge Committee to get permission, and that the head of the Committee, Mr. Whooping Crane, was very fussy about who could and could not go back as something different.

"Then," chimed in Miss Mouse, "you'll have to prove that you learned your lessons when you lived in the Green World. They are very strict about those sorts of things," she told him

"Lessons, what kind of lessons?" he asked them.

"Oh, the usual ones," replied Mr. Owl, "like being nice and thinking of others instead of yourself; doing good deeds, sharing and being honest; those sorts of things. Pretty easy stuff on the whole," said Mr. Owl. "Usually birds and animals don't have a problem understanding those lessons, but," he added, "it's surprising how many humans didn't seem to get them right. Humans are rather tricky creatures generally." Mr. Owl sighed as he stared out at the black sky with his great moon eyes.

"Oh, yes, deary me," squeaked Miss Mouse, "humans can be awfully difficult." Mr. Scootie nodded in agreement because he had never understood humans either when he lived in the Green World.

"How long will I have to wait before I can meet Mr. Whooping Crane?" Mr. Scootie asked Mr. Owl.

"Ah, that's the other tricky part," Mr. Owl replied. "It could take days or even months and sometimes it can take years, my dear boy; they are frightfully busy with issues like yours. Are you sure you want to do this? I mean go back as a bird instead of a dog?" Mr. Owl asked him.

"Oh, yes," Mr. Scootie replied enthusiastically. He could already see himself flying across the marshes, flapping his great wings and landing near a wild pony. "Oh, yes, I do, I do, I do." Then he jumped up and down and danced his twirly dance, until he got so dizzy, he fell down, and knocked Miss Mouse right off her feet.

"Gosh, steady on, dear chap," said Mr. Owl. "I'll go and have a word with Mr. Whooping Crane."

"Then what do I have to do?" Mr. Scootie asked him.

"Wait, I'm afraid," replied Mr. Owl, "you'll have to wait until they send for you. Then you'll have to fly off to their star for a few days. It's rather a cold star," Mr. Owl explained, but he thought that Mr. Scootie's thick white coat would keep him toasty warm.

"Why are they so fussy, what's so special about birds?" Mr. Scootie wanted to know. There was a long silence. Mr. Owl stared at Mr. Scootie, and his eyes got bigger and bigger until finally Mr. Scootie got a horrible attack of the shivvies.

"Birds, my dear fellow, helped make the Green World." Mr. Owl opened a wing and swung it around in a feathery arc.

"Pleeeesssee, don't do that," squeaked Miss Mouse. "You know it frightens me."

"I'm sorry my dear, I was just trying to show Mr. Scootie that like the trees, if there were no birds in the Green World it couldn't exist. We are brilliant creatures, absolutely brilliant," said Mr. Owl.

Mr. Owl then told Mr. Scootie that Mr. Whooping Crane could fly higher than the highest mountain in the Green World, and he added, "Most of us can fly as fast as those silly cars humans drive around in. We also fly thousands of miles each year. We all have to leave our homes when the weather gets too cold and so we keep flying until we can find a lovely warm place to live in. But," Mr. Owl said sarcastically, "unlike humans, who can't seem to get anywhere without a map, we use the stars and moon to guide us. Incredible feats, if I do say so myself." Mr. Owl spread out both of his wings and flapping them slowly, sang a little ditty.

Wings glorious wings, they are wonderful feathery things. They let us fly high up in the sky. Oh wings are such glorious things.

Brown Pelican

Mr. Owl added grandly that the Green World wouldn't survive without birds. "We pollinate the trees and flowers, and keep the place clean by eating bugs and insects. We work terribly hard you know. We are not in the least like lots of other creatures that never seem to work at all. Take lions for example," Mr. Owl paused, and gave out a loud sigh. "Lions spend their days lounging about under trees, and frankly once you've seen one lion you've seen them all. But not birds, dear boy, not birds. We come in all sorts of different sizes, shapes and colors, and we all sing different songs. My goodness, we really are spectacular." Mr. Owl puffed up his feathers and his large eyes glowed a brilliant yellow.

"Oh, pleeesssee, stop doing that," Miss Mouse squeaked again.

"I'm sorry my dear," replied Mr. Owl, "I'm awfully proud to be a bird as you well know. By the way," he asked Mr. Scootie, "how do you know so much about birds?"

Mr. Scootie then told them about the beautiful wild pony island he had lived on. He explained that it was covered with marshes and it was surrounded by a huge ocean that sometimes got so angry that it howled and screamed all night covering parts of the island with water. He also thought Mr. Owl would be interested to know that Mrs. Bean said that it was a very special place — because birds stopped there to rest when they were on the long journeys Mr. Owl had just told him about.

Mr. Scootie explained that there were so many different ducks with different colored feathers and different quacks, that he always got into a terrible muddle when Mrs. Bean tried to tell him all their different names. He told them that his favorite birds were the island ducks that waddled through everyone's gardens. And, he said, sometimes they liked to sit in the middle of a road for a quacky chat.

Mr. Scootie suddenly laughed, saying, "The visitors to the island would get so

Oyster Catcher

mad at the ducks that they kept honking their car horns hoping the ducks would move." "But," he said, still laughing, "the ducks never paid any attention and would just keep on sitting there, quacking away as the visitors shouted at them from their car windows." Mr. Scootie rolled back and forth on his back having an attack of the giggles, remembering it all.

He went on to describe the oyster catchers and herons, pelicans and ibis, bald headed eagles and — "Oh, enough, enough," squeaked Miss Mouse, covering her ears with her tiny paws. "They probably all eat mice," she exclaimed.

"Oh, don't be such a silly girl," said Mr. Owl crossly. "Water birds eat fish and crabs most of the time."

"What do you mean most of the time?" demanded Miss Mouse, giving him one of her hard beady-eyed stares.

"Well, sometimes they might eat the odd mouse," admitted Mr. Owl. Whereupon, Miss Mouse immediately tried to scamper away, and she would have succeeded if Mr. Owl hadn't caught her tail, with one of his sharp feet, and dragged her back.

"Oh, why do you have to do that?" she cried.

"Well, said Mr. Owl crossly, still holding onto her tail, "you've got to stop feeling so sorry for yourself. You seem to think that only mice have a hard time down in the Green World. Well, let me tell you my dear girl, so do birds. Living down in the Green World is very hard work for everything, especially birds."

"Do dogs work hard?" asked Mr. Scootie. Mr. Owl paused and gave out a long sigh before answering him. Finally he said that little dogs like him had a pretty easy time of it, and didn't do much work, but often bigger dogs worked jolly hard. "Doing what?" Mr. Scootie wanted to know.

"Well," replied Mr. Owl, "They help humans hunt birds and animals, they

Blue Heron

guard their sheep and cows, and often they guarded their homes as well; humans can't do things like that, for they have no sense of smell, poor things." Miss Mouse and Mr. Scootie laughed in agreement.

As the years marched along the three of them became best friends, laughing and joking with each other. Mr. Scootie flew back and forth to the island to visit with Mr. and Mrs. Bean. But as time went by, he also looked forward to coming back to his star, so that he could share his day with Mr. Owl and Miss Mouse. In fact he was so happy he'd forgotten all about the Knowledge Committee.

Then, one evening when they were busy entertaining Mrs. Zebra and a very smart fox, Mr. Scootie was laughing so hard that he didn't hear the loud wooshy sound, made by the largest and strangest looking bird, that suddenly landed beside Mr. Owl, blowing Miss Mouse right off her feet. Mr. Scootie was so frightened that he immediately got the shivvies so badly he couldn't move. The strange bird was covered with white feathers, and its beak was so long and curved that it looked like the branch of a tree, although Mr. Scootie couldn't really see the bird's head properly because its legs were too long.

Miss Mouse had vanished and Mr. Owl said in a very polite tone of voice, "Welcome, welcome, my dear Mr. Whooping Crane."

"Is this the little dog you told me about years ago?" inquired the strange bird.

"Yes, yes, it is," replied Mr. Owl.

"Pretty small dog I must say. I shouldn't think he's very useful," trumpeted the horrible monster bird.

"Oh dear, this is going to be awful," thought Mr. Scootie, still feeling frightened. "I wouldn't say he's useless," answered Mr. Owl. "He's a fine little chap. He made a family in the Green World very happy, and he still gives them lots of love and companionship. Most days he still flies down there to visit them."

"Well, the Committee will have to look into that," said Mr. Whooping Crane as he gave Mr. Scootie a nasty shove. "Ready?" he asked him in a deep trumpety voice.

"Yes, yes, I am," Mr. Scootie whispered. But his shivvies were so bad that he didn't know how he was going to fly across the sky to another star, following a bird with such big wings.

"Well then," said Mr. Owl brightly, "off you go. Good luck, my dear little chap. Good luck."

Mr. Whooping Crane gave Mr. Scootie another nasty shove which launched him out into the black sky. By twirling his little legs as fast as he could, he tried to keep up with the monster bird as it slowly flapped its great wings in front of him. Mr. Scootie was so terrified that it wasn't long before his legs went all wobbly. He was also so sure he would end up tumbling down to the Green World below, that he didn't see the blue star floating in front of him and crashed right into it. Yelping with pain, his legs collapsed, then he fell splat on his tummy and couldn't move.

"Thought you were pretty useless," said Mr. Whooping Crane, as he poked Mr. Scootie with his long beak and helped him stand up. But the star was so cold that Mr. Scootie couldn't stand on all four paws at once, so he had to do a little hoppity dance as he tried to follow the monster bird to the middle of the beastly cold star.

Then, as suddenly as it had appeared, the monster bird vanished, and Mr. Scootie found himself standing alone in the middle of a blue fog. Floating above the fog, he saw the heads of the strangest animals he'd ever seen. In fact, he didn't really know what he was staring at, because he had never seen such odd looking creatures before, and they were all staring down at him in complete silence.

"So, I presume you're the little dog who wants to go back to the Green World

as a bird?" growled an enormous tiger. Mr. Scootie couldn't answer because he'd lost his voice, and he was so cold he thought his teeth might rattle right out of his mouth.

"Now, come on; we don't have all day — answer the question please," roared another animal that looked like an enormous spotted Miss Peekaboo. Mr. Scootie could only nod his head, because he was too busy trying to sit on his tail, to keep his body from freezing.

"Why pray tell, do you want to change into a bird?" asked a nasty looking coyote, with sly and glinting eyes. Mr. Scootie opened his mouth again, but still no sound came out.

"Please answer them," whispered a tiny little red hummingbird that had suddenly appeared just above his nose. "Do try to be brave. I know how hard it is to feel small, but they only look frightening; they are really very nice," the little bird said. Then it darted off and vanished behind the blue fog.

"So, you're the little dog from the Purple Star?" said the nasty coyote again, baring a mouthful of vicious looking sharp teeth. "You've got quite a reputation I can tell you; fussy little thing aren't you."

"Well," the long necked camel sniffed, "he's one of those pampered little lap dogs they have down in the Green World, he's never had to rough it."

"Now, that's enough of that," said the huge monster bird who had suddenly returned. "I know you've all had a long day, but do try to be a bit nicer please."

"Oh, yes, yes, of course, so sorry," said the coyote sarcastically.

"So, Mr. Scootie, I hope you're going to tell us why you want to become a bird?" Mr. Whooping Crane trumpeted.

"Well," Mr. Scootie whispered. "Well. When I was in the Green World I saw this beautiful big bird every day. It was fishing and flying all over the marshes and I

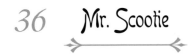
wanted, well, ur, I really wanted to be that bird. It looked so happy and free; I think I felt a little bit jealous that it could fly," he said as he sat back on his tail and shivered.

"That puts a stop to it right there," growled the tiger. "Jealousy isn't allowed up here; it always leads to destructive thoughts and actions, ending with very unhappy results for all concerned."

Phew — that sounded very complicated, thought Mr. Scootie. "I don't understand what you mean," he told the tiger.

"Well, jealousy," announced the enormous elephant. "Jealousy is when you are unhappy with what you have, and you think that if you can have the same things as someone else you will feel happier. But it's a trick, because everyone should be happy and grateful with what they already have, otherwise they will never find true happiness. These are very serious tests we all have to struggle with," declared the elephant, waving his trunk about in the blue fog, "and, if that's the reason you want to go back as a bird, then I'm afraid it's simply not on."

"Oh deary me," sighed the lovely panda bear. "For a long time this little chap wasn't happy in the Green World, and he did make a lot of changes when he went to live with Mr. and Mrs. Bean, giving them lots of love and happiness."

"And perhaps," chimed in the long necked kangaroo, "perhaps he was just dreaming of becoming a bird, instead of feeling jealous of it."

"Doubt it," growled the nasty spotted cat that looked like Miss Peekaboo. Then they all ignored him and began to whisper to each other. Mr. Scootie was so nervous he sat still as a rock pretending he was far away on his star with Miss Mouse and Mr. Owl. He was so busy with his dreams he didn't realize that all the animals had suddenly stopped whispering, and they were all staring at him in complete silence through the blue fog.

"Weelll," said Mr. Whooping Crane, in a voice that seemed to come from deep within the star instead of his beak. "Weelll, some of us seem to want to give you a chance. However," he continued, "we do have to know whether you tried to live by the four values? You do know what these are, don't you?" Mr. Whooping Crane jabbed his enormous beak back and forth and his eyes got very small and hard.

"Um, I'm not absolutely sure that I know what you mean," Mr. Scootie replied. "Mrs. Bean always gave me a biscuit if I did something special and good, and she would say she was very proud of me. Then, when I first saw the cats, I wanted to gobble them up; but I never did," Mr. Scootie continued.

"Now that's what we mean — we must be willing to make sacrifices for the sake of others, respect each other, work hard and be generous and brave," said the panda bear.

"Don't think he was very brave," trumpeted the elephant.

"Well, little dogs never are," snapped the nasty coyote again.

"Can I go back and live on my island near Mr. and Mrs. Bean?" Mr. Scootie asked them.

"Have to," the tiger yawned, as if he was bored with the whole subject. "After all," he continued, "that's where ospreys live. I am correct in saying that you want to become one am I not?"

Mr. Scootie was flabbergasted. How could the tiger possibly know what bird he wanted to become? He had never told anyone about his secret dream. Then he remembered that Mr. Owl had told him that the Knowledge Committee seemed to know everything. They could see the thoughts and actions of all the creatures in the Green World as well as the Golden World.

Mr. Scootie was so happy he jumped up on his hind legs and danced around

Osprey

in little circles clapping his front paws together. "All right, all right, stop all that dancing around, you're on your way to becoming a bird, so you had better start acting like one right now," said the camel firmly.

"But how do I become a bird?" asked Mr. Scootie.

"Don't worry," replied the kangaroo. "We take care of all those details for you. One day, when you wake up, you will have wings, that's all. Flying shouldn't be a problem, once you get the hang of it. You might get a bit hungry in the beginning; fishing can be a bit tricky, but if you watch the other birds, you'll soon figure it out. Now off you go," said the kangaroo.

Then, just as Mr. Scootie turned to leave, he heard the panda say, "Good luck."

And the little red hummingbird, that was hovering above his nose, said in a sweet little voice, "Follow me, I'll show you the way back to your star."

Mr. Scootie couldn't wait to get back and tell Mr. Owl and Miss Mouse what had happened. Miss Mouse thought it was dreadful that he was going to become a bird, and she started to cry. "Oh, do stop being such a silly little thing," Mr. Owl said crossly. Then, turning to Mr. Scootie he asked, "Well, dear chap, are you finally going to tell me what sort of bird you want to be?"

Mr. Scootie had dreaded this moment, because he was sure he was going to hurt Mr. Owl's feelings, but he knew he couldn't keep it a secret any longer. "I'm going to become an osprey," he announced.

"Good Heavens! Why didn't you tell me that before?" Mr. Owl cried out. "They are marvelous birds, great majestic creatures. I'd rather fancy being one myself to tell the truth. May I extend my congratulations to you and, when Miss Mouse can stop sulking, perhaps she'll be kind enough to feel happy for you too, won't you?" said Mr. Owl, giving Miss Mouse a hard stare with his huge yellow moon eyes.

"Oh, all right, if you promise you won't eat any mice down there," Miss Mouse reluctantly replied.

"Don't be so silly," said Mr. Owl, "he won't eat any mice; ospreys only eat fish." Then they all danced around in a little circle singing.

> *Hey. Hey. Hey — to a lovely Osprey. It's the dawn of a bright new day. Hey, hey, hey, to a lovely Osprey.*

It had been such an exciting and exhausting day that Mr. Scootie went straight to bed and fell into a deep sleep. Early in the morning he felt a strange sensation. At first he thought Miss Mouse was tickling his feet, but then he thought he was growing taller. He shook his head because he was still very sleepy, and he was sure he was just having another dream. But a few minutes later, he felt the same sensation again. Only this time he looked down at his feet, and to his horror he could see only two. "Oh, this is awful," he said as he watched his fur beginning to disappear and in its place were growing lots of blackish, brown and white feathers.

He began to panic, and thought once again, that if he had a good roll he'd feel better, and the dream would go away. But his body refused to turn over. Instead he began to float slowly above the purple hills, because by now two funny shaped feathery things were growing on both sides of his body. "Oh help," he said out loud. "I don't know if I want to be a bird after all. I must talk to Mr. Owl, I must, I must, I must." But every time he tried to land next to Mr. Owl, who was fast asleep, the big flappy things wouldn't let him.

The purple hills suddenly began to look smaller and smaller, until he couldn't see them at all. It was only then that Mr. Scootie realized he was really flying. "Oh my, oh my, I'm a bird!" he screechbarked.

And, just before he swept off the edge of the purple star, he was sure he heard a tiny little voice, squeaking into the wind saying, "Good luck Mr. Scootie. Remember, don't eat any mice down there." So he flapped and flapped his wings, hoping Miss Mouse would understand that he was saying goodbye, in the only way he knew how.

As he swept down toward the Green World he could see the water and the island with its green marshes spreading out like a gorgeous quilt beneath him. "Oh, this is marvelous!" he screechbarked again. "My dream has come true. I'm an osprey." Then, just as the wind caught his wings, sweeping him higher and higher above the great blue ocean, he suddenly wondered how he was going to let Mr. and Mrs. Bean know that he had indeed become an osprey.

As he flew further over the island he saw how small all the houses looked from upside down and he wished he could ask Mr. Owl why he could only see their roofs, and why the cars seemed like the little toy ones he'd seen children playing with. But the biggest puzzle was the humans. They were teeny little dots dashing hither and thither. Gosh, he thought to himself, he has so much to learn. Mr. Owl had been quite right — being a bird was clearly going to be "jolly hard work."

When he was a little dog everything had looked so big that he couldn't see the tops of lots of things. He couldn't even see human's faces if they weren't looking down at him, but now he could see only the funny looking hair on their heads.

Upside down life was going to be very tricky. Perhaps, he thought, if he made friends with another osprey it could tell him how to look for the roof of his old house, because he felt sure that once he found it, he would also find Mr. and Mrs. Bean. He knew that every morning Mrs. Bean always sat on her dock, wearing her purple hat while she watched all the birds flying back and forth across the cove.

Mr. Scootie gave out a loud screechbark of happiness as he imagined landing beside her on the bench, giving her a gentle peck on her cheek, then dropping a fish at her feet.

It was only then that he knew that he was going to have to learn how to perform special flying tricks so that she might pay attention to him. For a moment he longed to fly back to his star to have a chat with Mr. Owl, who seemed to have the answers to everything.

However, long ago, Mrs. Bean had taken him to a circus where they had acrobats. Funny looking men jumped up in the air, turning somersaults and flying all over the place like crazy birds. "That's what I must do," he thought; he could already see the surprise on Mrs. Bean's face when she looked up at him realizing that he had become an osprey. He could hear her laughing with happiness saying, "Mr. Scootie. Is that really you?" Then she would pick up the fish he'd dropped beside her and toss it in the air for him to catch. "Oh," he screechbarked, "life truly is wonderful."

And indeed it is.

About Mr. Scootie

Mr. Scootie, a Maltese, had been raised from a puppy by a loving family who had a child with severe health problems, and they could no longer keep him. It turned out that he and I shared the same birthday, so it was meant to be! He was the sweetest soul I'd ever known.

At walk time we would often go 'sploring. He'd jump on my lap in the car and off we would go, discovering previously unknown parks, rivers, coves and creeks. In the evenings, we'd sit on he dock watching all the hectic activity of the birds crisscrossing the island to settle into their preferred nightspots. Before bed, we always sat together, quietly listening to the water gurgling around the marsh grasses when the tide came in, while the ducks softly quacked away in the cove nearby.

He was not a brave little soul; sadly, our cats often caused him to get the *shivvies*. They made it clear that they didn't want him in *their* house. Mr. Huggybug, whose tail looks like a long black snake, would take great pleasure in rubbing it around Mr. Scootie, giving him a smack on the nose, and dashing upstairs. But it was Miss Peekaboo, who really gave him the *shivvies*. She would indeed hide, as her name indicates, then she'd jump out from behind a door or a piece of furniture, hiss and growl at him, then she'd vanish like a ghost in the night. I often wished that he could have barked and frightened them, even giving chase — but it was not his way. He was far too gentle a soul for such aggressive action.

I hope by writing this book, he will bring smiles and pleasures to others. I always believed that had he been human he would never have had a nasty thought about anyone or anything — except perhaps the cats.

About Chincoteague

Chincoteague Island lies five miles off the coast of Northern Virginia. It is seven miles long and three miles wide. The original inhabitants were indigenous Indians although little is known of them, except for the unique names they have left for the small towns along the Eastern Shore. In 1692 the colony was granted a charter from William of Orange, the King of England.

During the Civil War, Chincoteague sided with the North and was protected by a gunship called the Louisiana. It was during that time that the island became the primary supplier of oysters for New York City and other Northern cities.

Finally, in 1923, a bridge was built connecting the island to the mainland relieving the islanders of the isolation they had endured for so many centuries. Its population today is around 4,000 and the oyster and clam industry is the largest on the Eastern Shore.

Assateague Island is a thirty-three mile long uninhabited barrier island that protects Chincoteague and stretches along the pristine, undeveloped shores of the Atlantic Ocean. It also straddles the states of Maryland and Virginia. A lighthouse was erected on the Virginia side in 1833 to help sailors navigate the narrow shoals and today it still beams out to sailors and fishermen alike.

The origin of the wild ponies remains a mystery. Some people believe they came from a capsized Spanish galleon in the early 1700s, while others think that they might have been brought over to the island by the first settlers. It was established as a National Wildlife Refuge in 1943 to protect the abundant wildlife that migrates there throughout the year. Over 350 different species of birds stop to refuel on their long journeys to warmer waters.

Today, on the Virginia side, there are about a hundred and fifty ponies and an equal number on the Maryland side. Every year, on the Virginia side, during the last week in July, the "salt water cowboys" round up the wild ponies and swim them across the channel between Assateague and Chincoteague. The next day the ponies are auctioned off. This event has been going on since 1925 to raise money for a volunteer fire department after a fire destroyed much of the downtown area. It has now become so popular that it attracts thousands of people from all over the world, coinciding with a lively carnival.

Both islands have suffered devastating floods during their history as they lie only a few feet above sea level. In the 1800s a tidal wave swept a path of destruction and the extreme flooding of 1962 had a serious impact on Chincoteague and its economy. Since then, it has endured ferocious storms and hurricanes, and the winter of 2009 was particularly brutal, causing serious destruction to the beach and its dunes.

However, nothing can ever take away the great beauty of the islands. There is abundant wildlife, fishing and canoeing through the endless marshes filled with migrating birds. Each year in November, thousands of snow geese arrive settling in the marshes, and making them look as if a massive snowstorm had blanketed them during the night. With breathtaking sunsets dramatically reflected all around in the water, it is truly one of the most beautiful and peaceful spots to visit on the East Coast of the United States.

About Ospreys

Ospreys are one of the largest birds in North America with an average wing span of six feet, and they are found on every continent except for Antarctica. They eat only fish and are found near lakes, rivers and coastal areas like the Eastern Shore of Virginia, and Maryland and the Chesapeake Bay. Ospreys dive deep into the water, often almost disappearing, but once they have caught a fish with their long legs and sharp claws, they will orient it headfirst to ease wind resistance, making it easier for them to keep hold of their catch.

During the 1960s and 1970s ospreys became an endangered species until the pesticide DDT was banned in 1972. Since then they have slowly recovered. Now there are areas, such as Chincoteauge Island, where, with great joy, people can watch these magnificent birds flying across the coves and beaches, fishing and raising their young. They build large nests made with a variety of sticks and line them with softer material, such as seaweed or moss. They mate for life and the female, who is slightly larger than the male, will usually lay three eggs. Migrating ospreys return to the same nest year after year and have a life span of generally 25 years.

About the Author & Illustrator

Sarita Cooke was trained at the Chelsea Art School in London and completed her studies at The Museum School of Fine Art in Boston. She went on to become an abstract artist throughout the 1960s. In the early '70s, discouraged by the rapidly declining standards of the art scene, Sarita changed course and earned a degree in filmmaking from New York University.

However, in the late '70s, as a single parent, she once again turned her attention to art, painting portraits, using the difficult and unforgiving method of dry brush watercolor. She went on to win many national awards in this medium and painted portraits of interesting personalities throughout the East Coast. When she lived on Chincoteague Island however, she turned her attention to writing and contributed to *The Eastern Shore News* as well as the *Chincoteague Beacon*.

Mr. Scootie was inspired by a deeply personal experience when an osprey insisted on getting her attention as she was tending to the grave of her little dog. The osprey, not content with her response, followed her car until she stopped it, and winding down her window she wondered why it was being so persistent. It wasn't until she arrived home, on the other side of the island, that she realized that osprey was also making his presence known from the marshes outside her house.

It was this insistence of the osprey, and the fact that another one was sitting on the bridge as she drove toward the causeway one day, that she began to dream the improbable and, well, the impossible?

One thousand copies of *Mr. Scootie* have been published
by Osprey Island Press, Far Hills, New Jersey, in the
summer of 2010.

The text is set in ITC Galliard and the display type in
Boomerang. Composition and book design are by
Stephanie Ward of TeleSet, Hillsborough, New Jersey.